LAURENCE ANHOLT was born in London and brought up
mainly in Holland. His books have won numerous awards including
the Nestlé Smarties Gold Award for *Chimp and Zee*, the first story about
two lovable twin monkeys which he created in collaboration with his wife,
Catherine Anholt. Among his previous books for Frances Lincoln are
Can You Guess?, *Chimp and Zee*, *Chimp and Zee and the Big Storm*,
Monkey About with Chimp and Zee, *Chimp and Zee's Noisy Book*
(all illustrated by Catherine Anholt) and his Anholt's Artists series:
Camille and the Sunflowers, Degas and the Little Dancer,
Picasso and the Girl with a Ponytail, Leonardo and the Flying Boy
and *The Magical Garden of Claude Monet.*
Laurence lives with his family in a rambling farmhouse
near Lyme Regis in Dorset.

First published in Great Britain in 1994 by
Frances Lincoln Limited, 4 Torriano Mews,
Torriano Avenue, London NW5 2RZ
www.franceslincoln.com

This edition first published in 2006

British Library Cataloguing in
Publication Data available on request

ISBN 978-0-7112-2156-7

Printed in China

7 9 8 6

Visit the Anholts' magical bookshop,
Chimp and Zee, Bookshop by the Sea, 51 Broad Street,
Lyme Regis DT7 3SQ or shop online at www.anholt.co.uk

PHOTOGRAPHIC ACKNOWLEDGEMENTS
Please note: the pages in this book are not numbered.
The story begins on page 4.
Paintings by Vincent van Gogh (1853–1890)
Front cover: *A Wheatfield, with Cypresses* (1889),
National Gallery, London
Page 13: *The Postman Roulin* (1889),
Collection: Kröller-Müller Museum, Otterlo
Page 14 (above): *La Berceuse* (1889),
Museum of Fine Arts, Boston
Page 14 (centre): *Armand Roulin* (1888),
Folkwang Museum, Essen
Page 14 (below): *Roulin's Baby* (1888),
Chester Dale Collection, National Gallery of Art, Washington
Pages 15 & 16: *Portrait of Camille Roulin* (1890),
Museu de Arte de São Paulo Assis Chateaubriand.
Photograph by Luiz Hossaka
Page 28: *Vase with 14 Sunflowers* (1889),
Van Gogh Museum, Amsterdam
Page 31: *Self-Portrait with Grey Felt Hat* (1887–88),
Van Gogh Museum, Amsterdam

**For Cathy
With Love**

Camille
and the Sunflowers

A story
about **Vincent
van Gogh**

by **LAURENCE
ANHOLT**

F

FRANCES LINCOLN
CHILDREN'S BOOKS

WHERE Camille lived, the sunflowers
grew so high they looked like real suns –

a whole field of burning yellow suns.

Every day after school Camille
ran through the sunflowers to meet
his father, who was a postman.
Together they would lift down
the heavy sacks of mail.

One day a strange man arrived
in Camille's town. He had a straw
hat and a yellow beard. He looked
around with quick brown eyes.

"I am Vincent, the painter,"
he said, smiling at Camille.

Vincent moved into the yellow
house at the end of Camille's street.

He had no money and no friends.

"Let's try and help him," said
Camille's father.

So they loaded up the postcart
with pots and pans and old
furniture for the yellow house.

Camille picked a huge bunch
of sunflowers for the painter
and put them in a big brown pot.

Vincent was very pleased
to have two good friends.

Vincent asked Camille's father if he would like to have his picture painted, dressed in his best blue uniform.

"You must sit quite still," said Vincent.

Camille watched everything. He loved the bright colours Vincent used and the strong smell of paint.

He saw the face of his father appear
like magic on the canvas.

The picture was strange but very beautiful.

Vincent said he would like
to paint the whole family –

Camille's mother,

his big brother,

his baby sister...

and at last, Camille himself.

Camille was very excited – he'd never even had his photograph taken.

Camille took his painting into school.
He wanted everyone to see it.

But the children didn't like the picture.
They all began to laugh.

Then Camille felt very sad.

After school some of the older
children started teasing Vincent.
They ran along behind as he
went out to paint.

Even the grown-ups joined in.
"It's time he got a real job,"
they said, "instead of playing
with paints all day."

All that afternoon Camille sat watching Vincent work. It was very hot but Vincent worked fast. He painted the sunflower fields and even the sun itself.

'He is the Sunflower Man,' thought Camille.

"If I were rich, I would buy all your
paintings," he said.

"Thank you, my friend," laughed Vincent.

When Camille and Vincent came back
from the fields, some children from
Camille's school were waiting for them.

They shouted at Vincent and threw stones.

Camille wanted them to stop – but what
could he do? He was only a small boy.
At last he ran home in tears.

"Listen, Camille," said his father. "People often laugh at things that are different. But I've got a feeling that one day they will learn to love Vincent's paintings."

That night, Camille
had a strange dream.
He saw Vincent standing
in the moonlight
high above the town.

He had stuck candles on
his hat so that he could see.

The Sunflower Man
was painting the stars!

Early next morning, Camille was woken
by a loud knocking at the door.
Some men from the town had come
to see his father.

"Listen, Postman," they said.
"We want you to give this letter
to your friend. It says he must pack
up his paints and leave our town."

Camille slipped out through the back
door and ran down the street to
the yellow house.

It seemed very quiet inside.

Then Camille saw the sunflowers he had picked for Vincent – they had all dried up and died. Camille felt sadder than ever.

He found Vincent upstairs packing his bags. Vincent looked very tired but he smiled at Camille.

"Don't be sad," he said. "It's time

for me to paint somewhere else now.
Perhaps people there will like my pictures.

But first I have something to show you..."

Vincent lifted down a big picture.
There were Camille's sunflowers,
bigger and brighter than ever!

Camille looked at the painting.
Then he smiled, too.

"Goodbye, Sunflower Man,"
he whispered, and ran out of
the yellow house into the sunshine.

Camille's father was right. People did learn to love Vincent's paintings.

Today you would have to be very rich to buy one. But people visit galleries and museums all over the world just to look at pictures of the yellow house, of Camille and his family, and most of all, the sunflowers – so bright and yellow they look like real suns.

VINCENT VAN GOGH was born in Holland on 30 March, 1853. As a young man, he studied to become a clergyman like his father. He was 27 before he began to paint seriously. At the age of 35, Vincent went to the south of France looking for sunshine and brighter colours. Here he became friends with Camille's family. During this time he painted more than 150 pictures, although only one was sold in his lifetime.

Vincent became lonely and ill and at last, in a fit of madness, tried to cut off his own ear. He was taken to hospital, but even there kept on painting. In May 1890 he travelled north to Auvers-sur-Oise to seek help from another doctor. But only two months later he shot himself with a pistol. He died on 29 July, and was buried in the local churchyard, far away from the sunshine and colour he loved.

MORE TITLES IN THE ANHOLT'S ARTISTS SERIES

Degas and the Little Dancer

Marie wants to be the most famous ballerina in the world,
but it is hard to find enough money for the lessons.
So she begins modelling for the artist Edgar Degas.
When his beautiful sculpture *The Little Dancer*
is finished, Marie's dream comes true!

ISBN 978-0-7112-2157-4

Leonardo and the Flying Boy

Every day Zoro the young apprentice works hard in
Leonardo da Vinci's workshop. But there is one place
he is not allowed to go – a mysterious workshop where
Leonardo spends hours working away at a secret invention.
When Zoro manages to sneak inside, he is sent soaring
into an extraordinary adventure.

ISBN 978-0-7112-2132-1

Picasso and the Girl with the Ponytail

Shy Sylvette is astonished when Pablo Picasso, the famous artist,
chooses her to be his model. As the pictures become larger
and more extraordinary, Picasso helps Sylvette to be brave
and realise her dreams.

ISBN 978-0-7112-1177-3

The Magical Garden of Claude Monet

When Julie crawls into a mysterious garden, she meets
an old man tending the flowers. The gentle gardener turns out
to be the great artist Claude Monet and together they explore
his magical world. Monet and Julie wander across the
Japanese bridge, around the house and studios, and they float
through water gardens where lilies sparkle as bright as stars.

ISBN 978-1-84507-136-3

Frances Lincoln titles are available from all good bookshops.
You can also buy books and find out more about your favourite titles,
authors and illustrators on our website: www.franceslincoln.com